Overclocked

C.R. Allen

ONE

Mikey ascended the rotting stairs of his cold, dimly lit basement; they creaked and bent under each footstep. At the top, he paused only to hit the light switch. The room plunged into darkness except for the ghoulish blue light of his computer monitor. Mikey could have lived upstairs, but had opted for the solitude of his subterranean oasis.

The linoleum tile of the main floor hallway had once been white, but decades of dirt and oil had turned them the color of sun-faded limes. He had to pass several doorways on his way out of the duplex. The first was a spare bedroom.

Boxes of junk, mementos, and collectibles that his mother had hastily packed up when the bank man had come calling lined the spare room. Piled from the floor to the ceiling, crude handwritten descriptions indicated their contents. Their old house in the suburbs had plenty of storage, their new home in the city did not.

The next door led to a kitchen where the trashcan overflowed with takeout boxes and styrofoam plates. The laminate countertops bore the marks of bronze rings, imprinted by hot pots directly taken from the stove and set down without care. These overlapping circles created a chaotic pattern, vaguely reminiscent of the Olympic Games symbol in its disarray.

There was a dirty bathroom in the hall, filled with moldy towels and stained porcelain. The faucet and showerhead both leaked. The property management company's promise to fix the fixtures was just as unreliable as their other promises.

Beside it loomed the master bedroom, its door perpetually closed. By day, it served as a somber sanctuary for Mikey's father, a place of solitary confinement where he retreated to sleep away the daylight hours before his night shift. This room, steeped in shadows, was akin to a grim, desolate cell, a stark symbol of a man whose existence was consumed by a relentless commitment to long hours and hard work.

The last doorway in the hall, before the escape to the outside world, was just an opening. Beyond it was a dark living room bathed in the light of a television kept on loop 24 hours a day. Crammed on the walls were display cases with little porcelain figures placed inside. Most were half empty. An unfortunate casualty of several 'lost' moving boxes misplaced by the discount moving company they had hired. Mikey had tried to make an insurance claim on it, only to find the company had no such insurance and a small claims court would cost more money than it would be worth.

A thin silhouette sat on the sofa facing away from the hallway, only the back of the head visible above the couch. The woman's hair was white and frizzy, like thick layers of sea foam had taken form on her scalp.

Mikey tried to sneak past without being noticed.

"Where are you going?" asked the frail female voice.

Mikey paused.

"Out," he said, knowing that would likely not suffice, but he couldn't think of anything more clever.

"Be careful," his mother replied, not bothering to turn her head. "The news said there was another gun fight in the city, rival gangs. What has this world come to?"

"I will, ma," said Mikey, happy that she hadn't grilled him on his would-be whereabouts like she used to.

It would have only been a few years prior that she wouldn't have let him leave the house at all without knowing the exact GPS coordinates of where he was going and a committed time for his return. But recently, with Dad forced to work nights and sleep all day; her depression and loneliness had overtaken her. She had grown apathetic to anyone and everyone, resigned to make vague platitudes about the world falling into ruin around them.

She had always been an obsessive-compulsive personality, evidenced in her various porcelain figure collections she used to procure and maintain. But the run of bad luck, the poverty really, had broken her. Her only solace was the endless cable newscasts, watching with eyes wide open in an almost comatose state.

She used to shower Mikey with hugs and kisses, regardless of if he was going away for five days or five minutes. He used to return home to a house filled with the scent of something roasting in the oven. But since the move, Mikey hadn't seen his mother cook a proper meal. Their diet had devolved to primarily TV dinners and ramen, a fare that might have sufficed during his college days. Yet, as he matured, there grew within him a deep longing for the relatively sophisticated flavors of his mother's homemade meatloaf.

Not that he felt he was being picky; between his mother's meatloaf and foie gras, he'd take the meatloaf any day.

As he opened the door, the brisk chill of the night air hit him. He pulled his gray hoodie up to cover his face and stepped onto the city sidewalk.

The streetlights overhead cast an eerie glow on the concrete. With the moon still hiding behind the horizon, each beam of light from the high-pressure sodium lamp was like a stage spotlight, the gaps between lamps felt as dark and empty as the void between stars in the cosmos.

He had crossed over into the dangerous part of the city, a chaotic soup of gang violence, drug-induced carnage, and a general feeling to any outsiders that they weren't in Kansas anymore. It was the part of town that badly needed social services, but anyone who wanted help was far too scared to set foot there. The evening news had a permanent block of time dedicated to whatever juicy, horrific, or heinous act had gone on the night before. The TV producer knew that this part of town would never cease to deliver premium content that latched onto his viewership's fear index.

Mikey, aka MikeMeister457, wouldn't have hazarded the trip if he wasn't being paid. He had initially refused the job, but when xxSugar-Sweet996xx had offered triple his usual rate to venture from the safe confines of his basement for a house call on the wrong side of town; his pathetic bank account balance had compelled him to face the danger.

He had come prepared. The taser in his pocket was the safest counter-measure he could muster. With the city council's strict gun laws in place, getting caught by law enforcement with a firearm was likely to land you in jail. That didn't stop the criminal elements from carrying them. It only made their occupations as rapists, thieves, and murderers all the easier. Like everything in the world, nothing seemed to work like it should.

As he walked, Mikey pondered what had gone wrong. His parents had worked every day of their lives just to afford a house in a pleasant suburb with decent schools and green parks. It wasn't a lavish living, but it was a good living. Meals were warm, Christmases were joyous, and Mikey would have had the perfect child-hood. Then his dad's company went under and they suddenly didn't have any income while their stock investments almost evaporated before their eyes.

When the government handed out truck-loads of money to the big banks like candy on Halloween, Mikey had thought it was to help them avoid foreclosing on people's houses. Money was the problem right? They didn't have enough to cover their costs; so we gave them more, a lot more. Of course, that money came from the taxes on the people who lived in the houses the bank owned; so for a minute Mikey thought it was like the government was reinvesting it back into the people.

He remembered the day his parents received the news of the foreclosure. Mikey was furious. How could this happen?

He dug through the internet until he found out that the bank that owned their mortgage had received almost $20 billion dollars from the government. What was all the money for if not to help people like them keep their homes?

Meanwhile, the millionaires who lost their jobs after years of record bonuses got to walk away with bronze, silver, and gold parachutes. They were probably sipping mojitos on the beach somewhere, reading the paper, and shaking their heads when they saw the headline that foreclosures had gone up another 20%.

"It's a shame, those poor people out there," they would say before ordering a refill from the waiter.

It was clear the system wasn't designed for his parents or for him.

Now Mikey's family lived in a rent-controlled duplex with a semi-finished basement. Their pipes leaked, cockroaches bred faster than they could kill them, and the property management company threatened to evict them every time they complained. For people who had obeyed the law, worked sixty plus hours a week, and paid taxes for almost a lifetime; it was a sour conclusion to the American dream.

Mikey had never been good at the old school thing, earning Cs in almost every subject except for computer science. Regardless, the guidance counselor had sold him on going to college, as she did every student. He tried it for a couple years, but his subpar grades only followed him and soon he dropped out; student loan debt was the only mark of achievement that he would take with him.

Just like his parents, he took what the world gave him and tried to keep going.

He took a job at a big box electronics retailer doing tech support. It paid little and the benefits were shit. He often had to do the cost-benefit analysis of going to the doctor or being able to buy groceries that month, but at least it helped him pay his portion of the rent and reduce the burden on his parents.

Like many in the new gig-economy, he started side jobs on the internet to make ends meet, usually paid in cash. Mostly he just built or fixed people's computers. Hardware was his passion, and building the biggest, fastest rigs that his clients could afford was what he enjoyed doing.

When xxSugarSweet996xx reached out to his personal email about a job (he wasn't sure how she had got his personal information), he re-acted with suspicion. Mikey usually only took jobs from people who were a friend of a friend or regulars on the various internet message boards he frequented. Yet he had never heard of her before, nor could he find any reasonable connection between them. She said she was a 'fellow hacker' but he could find no mention of her activities anywhere on the internet. In the circles of those who know how to surf the dark web, the ones without a record were either posers or the most dangerous. She wouldn't divulge specifics about what she wanted him for, but the money she offered up front con-vinced him to take the job.

As he reached his final destination, he wor-ried he was being set up.

Mikey had arrived at the address as instruct-ed. It was an abandoned-looking warehouse near the docks. He checked the instructions again map on his phone. He was definitely at the right address. However, the building had no lights on and many **NO TRESPASSING** signs put up all over. It looked condemned, not even the homeless daring to squat under its flimsy awnings or chipped brick columns.

He messaged his would-be employer.

MIKEY: HERE

. . .

XXSUGARSWEET996XX: GO TO THE ALLEY, MAKE SURE YOU WERE NOT FOLLOWED!!!!

Mikey found the alley and pulled the taser from his pocket. He had seen enough movies to not risk being caught unaware if this turned out to be a ruse. He checked the charge. It was at max and he was ready. A zap from that thing would send anyone sprawling to the floor.

He crept forward slowly, using the light on his phone to illuminate the dark corners and crevices. Discarded building materials lined the alley, abandoned when whomever bought the place for remodel realized it would never yield a return on the investment. Piles of torn and discarded pieces of drywall formed unintentional teepees and forts that a child would have a field day playing in, if not for the likeliness of asbestos exposure. Screws and nails littered the asphalt, jingling like coins when Mikey kicked them as he stepped.

It ended in a dead end, a brick wall that blocked what little light from the city lamps still dared to sneak into the alley.

This is bullshit, he thought to himself. Someone was having some fun at his expense.

He had enough. It was time to head home.

"Mikey right?" a woman's voice asked from behind him.

Mikey jumped, almost falling to the ground. Someone was standing only a few yards away, someone who hadn't been there when he had walked up.

"A little jumpy," the voice said.

Mikey turned to find a woman standing there, the lights of the city silhouetted behind her. She was short and wore a purple hoodie, gray sweatpants, and sensible sneakers. It was difficult to see her face under the hood, but Mikey could make out a few distinguishing features; black lipstick, a nose ring, and strands of curly pink hair that spilled down her neckline.

"Are you SugarSweet996?," Mikey asked, trying to calm down with several deep breaths.

"Call me Rachel," she motioned towards a
dumpster against the wall. "This way"

Reaching around the side, she fiddled with
something behind it before attempting to push
it.

Mikey was confused. The dumpster was full
of scrap metal and trash, probably weighing
hundreds of pounds, yet it slid to the side with
ease. As it moved away, a chain pulley became
visible along with a doorway that led to a de-
scending stairwell.

"Come on, before someone sees," she said,
before disappearing into the subterranean
passage.

Mikey followed, compelled by his own curios-
ity and attraction to the mysterious girl.

He had hardly descended more than a few
steps when a motor sputtered to life and the
dumpster in the alley slid shut behind him.
The stairwell continued further down, barely
illuminated by lights at the foot of each step.

When he had reached the bottom and the path lights ceased to guide him further, he stood at the edge of the threshold to a room consumed in complete darkness but whirring with life.

His eyes were just beginning to adjust when bright lights flickered on around him. He was in what would have been the building's underground parking garage, thick brick columns holding up the ceiling and structure above. Glancing at the cracked and crumbling ceiling gave him little confidence that this was a safe place to be when it looked like at any moment, the entire building would fall on top of them.

"It's safer than it looks," Rachel said as she walked in front of him, sensing his trepidations.

Rows of computer towers, only a few feet of walkway space in between each, lined the room. Thick plates of glass housed them, like floor to ceiling aquariums except circuits and lights stared back at you when you peered inside. Thick bundles of wires seemed to spring from every corner of the hardware, arranged like a drunk spider's web; they zig zagged and crisscrossed the ground. He had to be careful not to trip on them as he followed the girl.

It was cold. Large refrigeration units against the outer walls hummed incessantly, sounding like competing swarms of angry bees warring against one another to see who could be loudest.

"This way," Rachel called from down one of the long rows.

Mikey followed, his eyes wide in amazement. LED lights of all sizes and colors blinked across the thousands of circuit boards and connection hubs. It was more towers than he had ever seen in one place before, a secret underground data center where no one would ever think to look.

They reached the end of the row, where an immense L-shaped desk sat topped with several laptops and at least a dozen monitors attached to arms hung from the wall. Some displayed black backgrounds with multi-colored lines of code arrayed into long strings. Others showed CCTV footage of the building's surroundings, like the street and alleyway.

"So you're probably wondering why I brought you here," Rachel said, sitting in the black mesh swivel chair at the desk.

"Kind of," Mikey replied, putting his hand into his jacket pockets. His fingers were getting numb.

"I checked you out," Rachel continued. "Thoroughly."

Mikey pondered what that meant.

"You seem like a decent guy," Rachel said, spinning around in the chair before facing him again.

"Thank you," Mikey said, not sure what else he should say.

"Hardware guy, I mean," she clarified. "Someone who knows how to take care of his tech. The help I need right now."

"You seem to have it under control," Mikey commented, gesturing towards the labyrinthian maze they had just walked through.

"I do, but that's all I have time to do anymore," she said with a sigh. "I need someone who knows their way around this kind of stuff to help me out."

"So that's the job?" Mikey asked.

"Pretty much," Rachel replied.

Mikey considered the situation for a moment. Something about it didn't feel right to him: the strange location with the James Bond villain lair vibes and the walls of towers pushing out immense computing power for god-knows-what. However, as he moved his hands around in his empty pockets to keep them from shivering, he thought about how little money he had left in his checking account.

"When do I start?" Mikey said, forcing himself to sound bought in.

"Slow down there, speed racer," Rachel said, standing up. "We have to lay some ground rules."

"Sure," Mikey replied.

"First," Rachel continued. "You see my workstation here?"

"Ya," Mikey said.

"You are never, ever, ever, ever, ever to touch it," she said with a stern face. "You aren't to sit down at my desk, you aren't to look at my screens, you aren't to do anything in this general area at all, ever. Is rule number one clear?"

"Ya," Mikey answered. He could relate to being protective of one's own workstation.

"Great," she said. "Rule two, not another soul is to know about this place. No friends, no family, no girlfriend, no boyfriend; nobody is to know what you are doing or where you are doing it."

Mikey paused.

"Why not?" he asked.

"Rule three," she began without answering his question. "Don't ask questions."

Mikey was about to ask one when he stopped himself.

"Very good," she said with a wink. "Now that the rules are established, do you think you can abide by them?"

Mikey weighed his options.

None of this looked legit. Either she was some kind of spy for a foreign government or a cyber terrorist. However, as the government hadn't really been doing him or his family any favors lately and corporations only looked out for their shareholders; his need to pay the electricity bill overpowered his need to have a clean conscience.

"I'm in," he said.

"Great, let's get started," she replied. "This way."

She led him along one row, which Mikey recognized as filled with server towers.

"Most of these are just to give me enough bandwidth to run what I need to on the web," she said as they strolled.

"Bandwidth to…" Mikey stopped himself when he noticed Rachel glaring at him.

"They need general maintenance, nothing special," she continued. "Just keep them from getting bogged down when my program is running."

Her program, the way she said it, almost guaranteed it to sound mysterious.

They reached the end of the row, where a steel door awaited them. She pulled a key from her pocket and handed it to him.

"This is where the proper work is," she explained as she pulled a second key from her pocket and used it to unlock the door. A loud hiss escaped as it unlatched. Fog emanated from the cracks in the doorframe.

As she slowly opened the heavy door, bright white light illuminated the mist.

It took Mikey's eyes a second to adjust, but eventually he could see that it was only a small closet. From the lines that ran on the walls, he could tell it was retrofitted with its own separate refrigeration unit, its own backup power supply, and special high output LEDs that bathed every surface with white light like a scene from an operating table at a hospital. On a stand in the center was a single computer tower, only four feet tall.

"All that out there," Mikey said with confusion. "And only this little guy to use it?"

"She may be small, but she is mighty," Rachel said with a grin. Her eyes flashed with strange affection for the PC tower.

Mikey sympathized with the feeling. His own rig at home was much larger and more impressive looking. When he had considered selling it for parts in order to make ends meet, it was akin to considering the selling of a child into servitude, and he hadn't allowed himself to do it.

He knelt on the cold floor and examined what he would be dealing with.

"I've been tweaking it best I can," Rachel said. "Really pushing the hardware to the limit but haven't been able to get very far."

"I see how you re-aligned these to better optimize it but you're still wasting capacity on the backend," Mikey remarked, examining the motherboard's configuration.

"See, I knew you were the right guy," she added.

"What kind of program are you trying to run on it?" he asked, as he fiddled with several wires.

"Rule number three," Rachel reminded him.

"I know," Mikey said, standing up. "First rule of fight club is you don't talk about fight club. But how can I optimize it if I don't know what you're doing with it?"

Rachel didn't answer. She stood behind him silently.

"I don't care what you're doing personally," Mike explained as he fiddled with the electronics. "You could be some spy or a terrorist. So long as your money is good, I'm your man. But if I'm going to be effective at my job, I'll need to know what it's running."

"I can't tell you," she added with hesitation. "Because it's not done yet."

"How about just the general idea, then?" Mikey asked.

"Ok," she paused as she considered how to answer. "It's an A.I. program."

Mikey turned his head and raise an eyebrow at her.

"It'll change everything," she added.

"Well then, I only have one last question," Mikey stated.

Rachel glared at him.

"Where's the bathroom?" he asked with a wink.

Rachel laughed.

"It's this way, next to my station," she replied.

"Great," he said, following her towards it. "This cold air makes me have to pee."

Two

For the next six months, Mikey would go to his day job at the electronics store, answering bullshit IT questions that bordered on idiotic; 90% of his job being instruction on how to turn the customer's computer off and then back on again. However, it allowed ample time during the day for him to research and plan how to optimize Rachel's mysterious rig. Then he would sneak over to the dangerous part of town after work and put in a few hours in the underground data center.

Rachel wasn't really a talkative person. They both worked quietly in their own areas. He would see her when he would take a leak, walking past her workstation with a nod and only glimpsing her program running on the screens. Otherwise, the only other times they would talk would be when he needed additional parts.

Money seemed to be no object for her. Whatever upgrades or replacements he recommended would magically appear the next day. She even let him take home any old parts that she no longer needed, adding to his collection of spare computer hardware filling up the boxes in his basement. Barely used and near top-of-the-line, he would be able to re-use them for other jobs and save some money.

He enjoyed it. Building the most powerful computer he could even conceptualize turned into quite the joyous experience. The hum of the servers was the only sounds he needed. The lights attached to his magnifying glasses guiding his steady hands as he maneuvered and soldered away into the wee hours of the night.

Every once in a while, he'd yell for Rachel to run a test and she'd report back. He had successfully pushed the processor speed, operating temperatures, I/O performance, and storage capacity beyond the original manufacturer's specs; overclocking them beyond what maybe even their original designers had thought possible.

Unfortunately, his life at home had deteriorated. His dad had been fired for not being efficient enough at picking and packing. A cable news show a week later highlighted how A.I. powered robots were replacing 80% of the workforce at the same location. The newscaster was almost giddy to trade banter with the company spokesperson about how great technological progress was. Progress, another term society uses to describe decommissioning old hardware (like his dad) and replacing it with the new and shiny. One look at the grungy box of parts in his basement reminded him of where obsolete hardware ended up.

They had to cancel all the streaming services in the house, limit their water use, and even start using their church's local food bank. Mikey was thankful he had the extra money from Rachel coming in, it was the only thing keeping the family afloat. Mikey had looked into moving somewhere cheaper, but to where was the question?

High interest rates kept rental prices sky high. If they moved out of town, he would have to quit working for Rachel, which had become their predominant income stream. They felt trapped, at least until his dad could find another job.

But another opportunity for him would never materialize.

It was a warm summer evening and Mikey was heading to work in what he had called 'the dungeon'. He had left his mom zombified in front of the TV at home. She was watching a news report about a crypto currency millionaire who had mysteriously disappeared with almost his entire company's holdings. Thousands of duped investors suddenly finding themselves broke. Next to her was Mikey's father, asleep on the recliner with an empty bottle of Jack Daniels still in his lap. His job search must have been going great.

He pushed these thoughts out of his mind as he hurried down the nearly abandoned streets near the dungeon. It was payday. That meant a thick envelope full of cash waiting for him. It wouldn't last long. Most of it would go to the property management company for last month's rent, then the water bill, then the electricity, and hopefully there would be enough leftover that he could bring home takeout for dinner the next day. With his mom in a virtually catatonic state, it would be a feast for them.

Mikey jumped when a police siren blared two quick bursts behind him. But it wasn't a regular police car, it was a black SUV; an undercover one with the lights hidden in the grill. He had been too distracted to notice its quiet approach.

The SUV pulled up beside him and the window rolled down. With the limited lighting on the street, the shadowed figures inside were only visible by their movements.

"Hands out of your pockets," said a deep voice.

Mikey felt nervous sweat forming on his brow.

Though he had so far avoided being arrested in his life, he had watched enough true crime shows with his mom to know what he was supposed to do when being ordered by law enforcement. However he also knew that fabricated evidence and innocent convictions happened often enough that whomever was in the vehicle, police or otherwise, could not be trusted.

"What are you doing out here?" the voice asked.

Mikey struggled to think of what to say.

"I asked you a question," the voice sounded annoyed.

Mikey was a terrible liar. He could only think about the envelope of cash waiting for him.

"Picking something up," he replied.

"Picking what up?" The voice pushed.

"I don't know," said Mikey, not able to think of anything believable to say.

"You don't know what you're picking up?" The voice asked with skepticism.

Mikey thought quickly. He had his backpack with him. It was empty in anticipation of bringing home old computer parts.

"They didn't tell me," he lied.

"Who didn't tell you?" The suit grilled him.

The moments felt like minutes as he tried to keep his cool and think of something that the suit would believe. He could feel the men in the SUV growing suspicions with each passing second. He had to think of something, and fast.

Mikey held up the phone in his hand.

"I work for Postmates," he said. "I just go where I'm told."

What a stupid thing to say. There was no way they would believe him.

Seconds passed, Mikey afraid to say or do anything.

He was ready for a half dozen police cars to appear out of nowhere, pull their guns on him, and arrest him for some unknown crime.

The passenger door opened, and a tall, athletic man stepped out of the vehicle. He wore a dark suit with a plain black nylon tie. His hair was dark and cropped tight to his scalp and despite it being well past sunset, he wore dark aviators that hid his eyes. In his mouth was a toothpick that swayed and danced between his lips.

"Have you seen a girl with pink hair?" the man asked.

"Who's asking?" Mikey said, not liking the man's appearance. He looked like he had just walked off the set of a Tom Clancy movie.

The man fished into his pocket for a moment and pulled out a black wallet that he flipped open into Mikey's face.

"Will that suffice, muchacho?" He said.

The FBI logo certainly looked real, not that Mikey had any way of telling a real one from a costume one. The man had his finger over the part that had the Agent's name and he pulled it back before Mikey could inspect the photo.

Mikey was about to ask to see it again when the Agent thrust a tablet in front of him. On the screen was a low-quality picture of Rachel taken from a CCTV camera.

"Know this girl?" The agent asked.

Mikey squinted his eyes, pretending to look closely.

"I don't recognize her," Mikey said after what he felt like was long enough to fool the officers.

"Are you sure?" The agent said. He didn't sound convinced.

Mikey took another long look.

"I mean," Mikey began. "It looks like a girl I knew in high school, except the eyes and nose are different. Same hair though."

A grunt of dissatisfaction sounded from the man.

"What do you want her for, anyway?" Mikey asked, partially because he was curious himself what Rachel had gotten herself into.

The agent put the tablet down and flicked the toothpick to the curb. Reaching inside the jacket of his suit, he pulled out another toothpick from the case and put it in his mouth.

"She's a terrorist," the agent said. "She's dangerous, has a weapon of some sort. It's imperative we find her before she slips away."

"Terrorist?" Mikey repeated.

"If you see her," the agent said, sounding dis-gruntled as he got back into the SUV. "Call 911 immediately."

"Do you want to give me your card?" Mikey asked. He still wanted to know the agent's name. "I can call you directly instead."

"No need," the agent said as the window rolled up. "We'll know."

The engine roared to life.

"Oh, and amigo," the agent said, rolling the window down a little. Only his glasses and bangs were visible in the narrow slat. "If I were you, I'd tell your pals at Postmates you couldn't find the place and get the hell out of here. It's about to get very busy in this neck of town."

The tires squealed as the SUV sped off, disap-pearing down the next street. The driver must have been punching it because Mikey could still hear it even after it was out of sight.

Mikey stood there, considering what to do next.

He wasn't sure if the agent believed him about the Postmates thing or about not recognizing the girl with the pink hair. But if he didn't believe him, why let him go?

Could it all be some FBI trick? They would arrest him later and force him to tell them the truth.

Except he knew nothing. Rachel hired him to do a job. That was it. Any attempts at questioning him about Rachel's past or present activities would yield a disappointing result for them. Her mysterious program was just that, something he knew jack about.

Mikey considered turning around and going home, but something stopped him. It was the assurance that if he went home, he would give up on their shot of catching up on rent. The laws weren't too favorable once you were 60 days past due. They could find themselves completely homeless in just a matter of weeks. It would be like when they were told they were being foreclosed on and had only a few days to pack up their entire house, their entire lives.

He looked all around him. There was no car on the street following him. There was no helicopter flying high overhead. He was standing alone on the pavement, just himself

Mikey would go in and get his last paycheck, then tell Rachel it was off.

He continued towards Rachel's underground data center. Thankfully, it took him in the opposite direction of where the SUV had turned. One more corner and he would be in sight of the abandoned building. A noise filled his ears, the sounds of police sirens approaching and quickly.

Not wanting to risk being caught in the open again by the Agent, he took the back way through the alleys to Rachel's place. It didn't take long before he could see the alley with the hidden door across the street.

Mustering up whatever courage he had, Mikey peered around the corner.

There was the abandoned building with over a dozen cop cars parked out front. The officers with their weapons drawn had their full attention trained on the building's boarded up front doors.

The cops were completely ignorant of the side alley entrance; it was unguarded.

Several more vehicles pulled up to the front, including a black armored van, men in SWAT gear piling out of it.

Mikey felt like he was in the middle of a Die Hard movie.

He slid back into the darkness of the alley, considering his decision to not beat it for home was already a poor one.

The sudden feeling that he was not alone interrupted his thoughts. Someone else was in the alley behind him and their footsteps were running towards him.

If he had been in an action movie like Die Hard, he would have been credited as inno- cent bystander number three. You know, the one who dies right after the opening credits because he was too damn slow.

Something hard hit the back of his head and he went sprawling to the ground, landing on the asphalt with a thud. Pain shot up his back.

"Shit, it's just you," a familiar voice said above him.

It was hard to make out who it was with the glow of the city reflecting in the night sky and forming a kind of halo around the person with the backpack standing over him. As his eyes adjusted he noticed a familiar twirl of pink hair dangling above his head.

It was Rachel.

"That hurt," Mikey said, still wincing in pain.

"Shh," she replied, helping him up. "We got to get out of here."

On his feet, he clutched at his lower back.

"What is that out there all about?" He demanded. "Are you in trouble with the government? I've got no interest in going to jail."

"Come on, let's get away from the street," she said, pulling him deeper into the alley.

He followed reluctantly. She was practically dragging him. It was almost surreal. The alleys around the dungeon were usually swarming with vagrants and street gangs. Tonight they were completely empty except for Mikey and Rachel. It was like the police action was a light shining into a sewer, and the cockroaches had scattered into the nooks and crannies to avoid detection.

"Goddamnit," she said in a loud whisper, setting her backpack on the ground softly. Apparently, she was comfortable with their distance from the road to speak again.

"A friend of mine at the FBI tipped me off this morning," she began. "Someone told them about what I was doing and where I was working."

Mikey looked at her, dumbfounded.

"Wasn't me," he said.

"No shit," Rachel replied. "I've been watching everything you do since you started. If it was you, I'd know already. I think it was my ex. She was a jealous bitch."

"You've been watching me?" Mikey asked in alarm, appalled at the invasion of his personal privacy.

"Shut up," she said, sounding annoyed. "My ex knew nothing about you, therefore they know nothing about you. Listen to me and do what I say and it'll stay that way."

"I don't know," Mikey said with a faltering conscience. "I really don't know what you were up to in there. Maybe I should turn myself in or something."

"Turn yourself in?" She said in disbelief, then started laughing. "Fine, suit yourself. Go let Mr. FBI agent, who thinks McNulty from the Wire is his hero, go to town on you in a closed door interrogation room."

Mikey imagined the agent he met earlier staring at him with that toothpick in his mouth, rolling up his sleeves, and cracking his knuckles.

"Can you even afford a lawyer?" Rachel asked.

Mikey turned bright red. If she was as good a hacker as he thought she was, then it was likely she knew everything about him, including his bank statements.

"They'll have you with a signed confession before the sun comes out," she added with a smirk.

"Confession," Mikey repeated with an ominous voice. "Listen, I don't want to get in trouble. I can't, my folks, they rely on me. My dad, he lost his job, if I go to jail..."

"You won't if you listen to me," Rachel said with determination. "But if you don't listen to me, you'll find yourself just another nameless face that gets fished up out of the river as I completely delete you from every social media site and government registry. The very memory of your existence will be as real as a 90s movie starring Sinbad as a genie."

"Shazam?" Mikey said.

She stared at him with eyes that could face down a tiger.

Mikey shut up.

"Thank you," she added. "You can't see it, but they have a perimeter around the area right now that no one could break through, not even me. And even if you knew something," she continued. "Which you don't. They'd still wail on you until you told them something incriminating."

Mikey felt a bead of sweat drip down from his forehead. He wasn't sure who he was more afraid of: Rachel or the Agent.

"There's no way out of here for me," she continued. "But there is for you."

"You're going to turn yourself in?" Mikey said, confused.

"Yes, but you're going to do something for me," Rachel replied.

"What's that?" Mikey asked.

She slid her backpack over to him.

"You take my rig," she said.

He immediately recoiled as if the pack was full of poisonous snakes.

"The evidence?" He asked in disbelief. "You want me to take the evidence?"

"You're going to take it," Rachel said. "Or we'll both end up in jail."

"I don't know." Mikey stroked his hair through his hands.

"Jail or not," Rachel continued. "I know you and your folks only got another month or two before you're out on the street."

"No, that's not entirely true," Mikey lied, even though he did not know why.

"Yes, it is," said Rachel, with a sinister calmness to her voice. "In the bag is $15,000 cash."

Mikey's eyes were wide.

"That'll give you guys at least six months before you're hurting for money again," she added. "You do this for me. It's all yours. Go ahead, check it."

Mikey hesitated, but something about the allure of a big wad of cash compelled him to unbuckle the top latch on the flap and peer inside. Nestled next to the rig, cushioning it, were thick bundles of cash neatly arranged in rows.

"I'd offer for you to count it," said Rachel, the faintest bit of concern showing in her voice. "But we are running out of time."

A helicopter with a searchlight flew overhead at breakneck speed. They both ducked.

"But what about all the servers?" He queried. "All the other equipment, it probably has..."

"Let me worry about that," Rachel replied, cool as a cucumber. "I just need that computer, that program, to be safe. Take it home, hide it in a closet. Don't tell anyone about it, not a soul. If you can do that, I'll pay you double when I come back."

"All that just to store your computer for you?" Mikey asked.

"Yes, just to hold it," she answered. "Do not plug it in, do not turn it on, do not use it. It's not ready yet."

"What if you don't come back?" Mikey asked.

"I will," Rachel said, but she sensed the doubt in Mikey's eyes. "My bitch of an ex may have told them what she knew, but without the program, it won't hold in court. By the end of the night, they won't have anything they can keep me with. If I'm not back in three months, destroy it and everything on it. It's too dangerous to be in anyone's hands but mine. Can you do that?"

"Yes," Mikey said. "I think so."

A rush of air blew through the alley as a black SUV passed it on the street at high speed.

Both of them remained silent, waiting to see if it would turn around or stop. It did neither; it had not noticed them.

"There is no 'think so' here, Mikey," Rachel said. Her eyes were very serious. "Can you do it?"

"I'll do it," Mikey said with as much confidence as could be mustered.

"Good," Rachel said, standing up. "I'm going to cause a diversion. You started heading home through the alleys. Understand?"

"Yes," Mikey said. "How will I get a hold of you if I need to?"

"You won't," she said, walking towards the street. She disappeared around the corner.

Mikey stood there, stunned for a few more moments.

He thought about leaving the computer and taking the cash home. It would clear him of holding any evidence and being marked as an accomplice. He could look for another side job, maybe something less nefarious this time.

The image of the wads of cash in the bag pulsated in his head like a heartbeat.

$15,000 was a lot of money, but Mikey knew deep down that even that much wouldn't last forever. By Christmas, they'd be behind again. He would need to fulfill his end of the bargain if he didn't want his parents to spend the new year living out of a suitcase.

He wanted to ask Rachel about the program, one last violation of rule number three. He rushed to the street and peered around the corner. In the distance was the abandoned building surrounded by cop cars. Rachel was halfway between him and them. She turned to him and winked before pressing a button on the phone in her hand.

What did that mean?

Mikey hit the ground as the shockwave from the explosion flew down the narrow streets. The abandoned building was a fireball. All the police officers were laying on the surrounding ground; knocked over from the explosion.

What did Mikey get himself into?

THREE

The end of summer hadn't gotten easier for Mikey and his parents. Rent was caught up, but in August his dad had a stroke. The medical bills had put them back at square one. Not having employer provided insurance in America is a dangerous gamble and one they had lost. Mikey had minimal benefits from the big box retailer, but they didn't extend to his father, who hadn't been able to afford Cobra insurance after being laid off.

Mikey had treated his parents to fast food for dinner that night, despite his father's doctor advising him to stick to a strict, healthy diet. Healthy food was expensive, and at this point it was a question of whether to eat healthy or pay the electricity bill. So an artery clogging cheeseburger with soggy french fries became the most efficient cost to calorie ratio available to survive.

Mikey was feeling guilty, morally torn over whether he had done the right thing helping Rachel. Her pyrotechnics display the last time he saw her had killed no one, only a few burns for the officers who were too close. But he hadn't helped her because she was innocent. He had almost no doubt in his mind that she wasn't. It was the money, the money his family needed so badly; that was why he was probably committing multiple felonies at this very moment.

But he needed something right now more than a clear conscience. He needed more money; money to get his dad the help he needed, money to make sure their home stayed theirs, money to eat something other than grease until they died from choking on it. Money was one thing he knew Rachel had plenty of.

However, he did not know how to get a hold of her. If she had turned herself in, would the FBI give her a phone call? Could he call the police station and ask? He erased the thought from his mind immediately. That would be stupid to arouse suspicions like that.

"Hi, I'm Mikey. Do you have a dangerous cyber terrorist in custody I could talk to?"

He and his family sat in silence on the couch with the news on. On the TV, they were reporting on a pharmaceutical executive who was being indicted for misleading consumers. His family was in the background in their designer clothes and wearing Rolex watches. The reporter commented they were looking to settle out of court with an agreement for several hundred million dollars. Mikey googled them to find they were worth several billion.

Likeliness of jail time, zero. Likeliness that they would be in danger of losing their home, zero. Likeliness that they would have to give up eating at 5-star restaurants in order to make ends meet, zero. Likeliness that their actions had directly led to the deaths of regular people, just like his parents, almost certain.

The reporter wouldn't shut up about how it was progress in the fight against corporate malfeasance. There was that word again, progress. Everyone on TV loved to say it, but none of them knew that it really meant to people like him.

The reporter passed segment to a couple talking heads, smiling like idiots on a so-called 'panel of exports'. One panelist was keen to point out that the family would have gotten away with it if it hadn't been thanks to a whistleblower who had given the FBI one of the company's laptops with the damning evidence. Another talking head, one of those personalities who get paid more when they say something controversial, demonstrated that the whistleblower wasn't a hero. They would be due 30% of the monetary sanctions garnered in the case. They'd be overnight millionaires, so maybe they weren't doing the right thing after all and were just doing it to get rich.

Mikey felt disgusted when the heads nodded in agreement. A single family makes billions off of selling dangerous products, and they are more concerned about the intentions of one person who stands to make millions off of turning them in for it?

As he looked at the fast food wrappers that littered the living room's scratched and worn coffee table, the gears in his mind turned.

If he waited for Rachel to contact him and give him the last payment, it would get them through a few more months. He could try to blackmail her for more money, but it would never be enough to get them out of the hole they were in. That was if she even came back at all. She might be holed up in Guantanamo Bay or some other black site, forgetting what the sun looked like. Hell, she could be getting waterboarded at this very moment by Mr. FBI agent; inches away from spilling the beans on who and where her computer was.

Whereabouts that, if she divulged, would lead to a raid of his home and his own incarceration as her accomplice. She might even try to pin the whole thing on him. Cop shows talk all the time about how possession is nine-tenths of the law and Mikey was the one still holding the computer.

On the other side of the equation, maybe something on her computer was valuable. A piece of insider information on a corporation that could qualify him to the government as a whistleblower. If not to the government, maybe something that someone on the internet would pay top dollar for. Either way, he needed to know what he was holding before he could determine what to do next.

"I'm going downstairs to work," Mikey said, excusing himself.

His dad grunted a goodbye, having lost most of his ability to speak since the stroke. He sat in his chair with his one still good arm clutching tight to the bottle of bourbon. Mikey's mother didn't even hear him, her eyes glued to the news report. The news anchor's reflecting in her dull, dead eyes.

Mikey walked down the stairs to the basement, his own scaled-down version of the dungeon. His mind was resolute, he had to help himself and his folks. They needed money and they needed it now. That computer was his only ticket.

Pulling it from the closet where he had hidden it under piles of spare computer parts; he plugged it into a wall outlet, ran an HDMI cord to his monitor, plugged in an ethernet port, and inserted his wireless keyboard-mouse dongle to the USB port.

Taking a deep breath, he hit the large circular power button on the tower and the fans whistled to life.

As the processor whizzed and the immense cooling fans spun, Mikey expected Linux or Windows to pop up. When it did not, he thought maybe something was wrong.

All that appeared on the screen was a command prompt screen, but it wasn't MS-DOS. It was blank, with no instructions or commands. He thought for a moment and then tried something.

Hello, he typed.

Three dots appeared on the screen and followed by.

Hello, it responded in purple lettering and a different font.

Rachel had mentioned it was an A.I., so just a program designed to mimic human intelligence.

What are you called?

Three dots showed it was thinking, then disappeared as it typed back.

`Artificial Cognitive Technology for Interactive Operations and Networking. But you can call me ACTION.`

"Cool," Mikey said out loud with a sarcastic tone as he rolled his eyes.

Did a four-year-old think of this acronym? It sounded like something so devoid of inspiration that the program itself probably had thought it up.

What can your programming do?

`I am designed to complete queries from users.`

"Ok then," Mikey said aloud to the screen.

He thought about how he could use it to his advantage. Maybe it had Rachel's information stored and some kind of way for him to track her down for more money.

What's my contact information?

The three dots lit up and then faded. It had finished the request and was typing.

His jaw dropped. The program was spitting onto the screen a complete list of emails, phone numbers, aliases, current and past addresses; except they weren't Rachel's. They were his.

Mikey checked the tower. There was no camera on it. How did it know he wasn't Rachel?

It probably just read the IP address and pulled his information up off the web. It was a clever way to establish who the user was.

Would you like to start a query?

He had only played with A.I. a little thus far, finding them a little too rudimentary in their capabilities and use-cases to be of real value. He tried a prompt that he saw online.

Make me the perfect martini.

The three dots returned to the screen as the algorithm went to work to find the most human-like response to the question.

Mikey waited. And waited. And waited.

Looking at his watch, three minutes had elapsed and still it had yet to reply.

He thought maybe it had hit an error and needed to be reset, but there were no icons on the screen to stop generating the response or start a new one. There were no other options available except to wait for it to finish thinking.

Maybe Rachel wasn't all that she had cracked up to be. This ACTION program was even worse than what he could find for free on the internet. It would need a lot more work before it could be of value to anyone, especially him.

He immediately felt disappointed. When life had given him a glimmer of hope, it proved to be just another mirage. There would be nothing special about this computer, except for whatever he could get for trying to resell the parts.

Mikey walked up the stairs back to the living room, his shoulders sunken in defeat. He didn't even bother to unplug ACTION, its three little dots still blinking on the screen.

He was understanding why his father had drunk himself to a passed out stupor so many nights, or why his mother cared more about the events on the evening news than those of her son's life. When life had dealt you shit hands of cards over and over and over again, it was easier to just stop playing the game.

Sitting next to his mother on the couch, he lost himself to the generic police procedural playing on the network television. They had cut the cord to save money and the old antenna on the roof was their only way to watch television anymore.

So while ACTION was busy pushing their internet bandwidth to its limit, he was none the wiser.

Four

H e awoke on the couch to the front door buzzing. His parents had gone to bed, leaving him alone with the TV tuned to after hours paid programming. The type of infomercials for miraculous cooking ovens and cleaning detergents that taunted insomniacs desperately unable to sleep. The door buzzer went off again, this time in two short bursts, the person on the other end was growing impatient.

Mikey groggily stood up and went to the entrance. Not wanting to open it for whatever drunk had mistakenly come knocking, he peered through the peephole.

Standing on the other side of the door was a man dressed in a tuxedo, holding a silver tray.

Mikey was confused.

He pressed the intercom on the door.

"I think you have the wrong address," he said.

"I don't think so," the tuxedo-clad man replied. "Is this…"

He read out Mikey's name and residence exactly.

Mikey opened the door.

"I don't know what game you're playing, buddy," he said, but stopped.

"Your martini, sir," the tuxedo man said, presenting the tray to Mikey. Sitting on the tray was a glass with an olive in it. "Made exactly to your specifications."

Mikey's confusion doubled, so much so that he couldn't help but laugh.

"I didn't order a martini," he said.

"Sir," tuxedo man replied with a snooty attitude. "I was paid handsomely and given very specific instructions on how to make this martini, along with who and where to deliver it to. Please sir, so I may be on my way back to BarFly."

"BarFly?" Mikey remarked. "That fancy place downtown?"

"Indeed, sir," tuxedo man said. "I am the head bartender and my absence is sorely missed. So if you would please."

He practically shoved the tray into Mikey's face.

Not knowing what else to do, Mikey picked up the glass from it.

"Thank you," Tuxedo man said, bowing. "Have a pleasant evening."

He turned and quickly disappeared into a waiting car.

Mikey remained standing in the doorway, holding the drink, unsure of what had just happened. It wasn't until he noticed a passing neighbor walking their dog, staring at him, that he closed the door.

Carefully carrying the drink down the stairs to his basement, he went to the computer, which was still running. However, the three dots had vanished and a response from AC-TION was waiting for him.

Were the results of the query satisfactory?

Mikey took a sip. It was indeed very good. However, he had never had a martini before, so he wasn't sure what it was supposed to taste like. Based on this one, he could definitely go for more like it.

He typed his response.

How did you do that?

`The perfect martini in itself is unattainable, as it is based on the subjectiveness of the observer. I cross-referenced your preferences for food and drink with your ancestry results and other demographic factors to identify the martini recipe most likely to satisfy your flavor profile. Then I located the closest bartender to you that had both the supplies on hand and skill level necessary to prepare it and paid them the necessary amount to fulfill said request.`

Mikey couldn't believe it, but concern immediately entered his mind.

There's no way I could afford however much you paid him to make that.

While performing the query, I performed several million trades on the Tokyo Stock Exchange on your behalf that yielded a net gain to cover the costs of your query. You find that the $1.73 I removed from your bank account in order to perform these trades has been returned, plus any additional gains obtained.

How much additional gains were there? $127.43 USD.

Mikey felt like his jaw had hit the keyboard. There was no way this was correct. This was a fantasy. He pulled out his phone and immediately accessed his bank statements.

His checking account had $159.67 USD in it. He checked the transaction history, a recent one subtracting $1.73 immediately after he had started the query with ACTION and $1 27.43 being deposited back in shortly after.

How did you get access to my bank account?

I was able to successfully guess your password using publicly available information.

Mikey found this statement very alarming.

But I have two-factor authentication turned on.

I was able to gain access to your mobile device after submitting a simulated federal request to your telecom provider under the pretense of monitoring you for criminal activity.

Mikey looked at his phone and saw the one-time authentication code in his text messages, all marked as read.

Mikey collapsed into his computer chair and drank the last of the martini in one big gulp.

Maybe Rachel was all she had cracked up to be after all.

Would you like to start another query?

Mikey woke up the next morning, uncertain if the fancy waiter at the door had all been some crazy dream. The alarm on his phone blaring in his ear was not and he grumpily got ready for work. In the shower, where the water was always lukewarm at best, he drifted off to thoughts about what he would ask ACTION to do next. Losing track of time, he had to rush to get dressed, as he was risking being late for work at his day job.

Passing by the kitchen, he stopped dead in his tracks when he saw his mother sitting at the small kitchen table crammed between the cabinets and the shared wall with the neighbors. Despite his urgency, he knew this change of scenery for her was a big deal, so he entered and approached slowly. When he was close enough to hear her sobs, he rushed forward to hug her.

"What's wrong ma?" He asked.

"Nothing honey," she lied, trying to wipe her tears with a dishcloth. Mikey knew she was lying. Her eyes were so tired and red from the tears that any chance she had of passing it off would be futile.

"It's dad, isn't it?" Mikey said.

Her sobs intensified.

"The Doctor called," she said as best she could muster. "Your father didn't make the cut for the trial."

Mikey had found a breakthrough medical trial for people who had suffered catastrophic strokes while researching on the internet. It had always been a long shot that he would be chosen, they knew that when they applied, but the gut check of the final rejection pierced deep, regardless.

"Don't you have to get to work?" She said in between sobs.

Mikey looked at his phone. If he didn't leave now, he would be late.

"Don't you worry about us," his mother said with a smile that did little to reassure him. "We'll be just fine, your father and me. Our luck has to change at some point."

Mikey hugged her, then slipped out towards the front door, but he never made it past his hand on the doorknob.

Our luck never changes, he thought to himself.

He wasn't wrong. As long as he'd been old enough to understand, their family seemed cursed with ill-fortune. Waiting around for the world around them to change in their favor hadn't worked, but maybe Mikey could do something about it.

He ran downstairs, typed a short sentence into ACTION and pressed enter almost without thinking.

His boss made a big deal about him being late, threatening to do a formal write-up and send it to corporate. Mikey just nodded, thinking the man was so caught up in the corporate handbook he probably read it to his kids at bedtime.

In the end, his boss would forget all about it. The man was quick to jump onto a high-horse as the manager and talk down to an employee, but once he disappeared into his back office to read company emails and other busy work for a few hours, it would be like it never happened.

The day dragged on, Mikey going through the motions, but his thoughts were not far from his mother and father. After what felt like an eternity, it was time to go home.

Walking through the front door, he was startled when someone almost tackled him as soon as he entered. The frail frame of his mother wrapped its arms around him and squeezed him tight.

"You won't believe it," she exclaimed. "The Doctor called back. They got more funding, they could expand the trial, and your dad got picked this time!"

"That's amazing," Mikey replied as his mother let him go. "Where's dad?"

"In the living room," she said, the tears of joy streaming down her face a stark contrast to the ones of despair she had that morning.

Mikey found his dad on the recliner, a beer in one hand.

"I see you started celebrating without me," Mikey joked.

His dad grunted in reply. Since the stroke had paralyzed most of his face, it was about the best he could muster. Mikey patted his father's thin bony arm, it felt so skeletal even under a thick layer of flannel.

Mikey stood up.

"How about a treat tonight?" He asked them both, hoping to elicit another grunt of approval from his father. "How about a nice hot pizza from our favorite place? To celebrate."

He was partially concerned his parents had been cutting back on meals too much in order to cut costs. Both looked painfully thin.

"That's a great idea, honey," Mikey's mother said, but the glint of excitement in her eye faded slightly as she shifted her tone. "But I'm afraid we shouldn't risk it. Though the treatments are covered by the trial, there'll be extra transportation expenses and a special diet they'll have him on. We should save our money until then."

"My treat, ma," Mikey said, not wanting to ruin the moment. He fished into his pocket to pull out some cash, but his mom shook her head at him.

"Save it for rent, dear," his mother said. "For now, let's just cherish what we received today. A stroke of good luck."

"Luck, right," Mikey said as he descended the stairs to his dungeon. ACTION's screen greeted him.

Would you like to start another query?

He thought about asking ACTION what it had done, how it had gotten the clinical trial to get his dad accepted. Yet he refrained. Sometimes it was best not to ask how the sausage gets made.

His stomach rumbled. Just the mention of pizza had subconsciously made him feel much hungrier than he was. Like a man stranded on a deserted island, who had grown accustomed to a meager sustenance but grew ravenously hungry at the mere dream of actual food.

He thought about asking ACTION to get him and his family a pizza.

The program just got his father admitted to a medical trial, and Mikey suspected it could do much more than that. And all Mikey could think of to do with it was to order the delivery. He almost felt ashamed for being so shortsighted.

The problem was money. It was always money.

He logged into his banking app and checked his account. It was growing dangerously low again, and he wasn't due for a paycheck from work for another week and a half.

An alert popped up on his phone. It was a new email from a friend asking if he could build them a new computer. Mikey felt temporarily relieved. It wouldn't pay much, but it would help.

The rest of the night, he gathered the spare parts and got to work. With his soldering gun in hand, he weaved together what he had until it fit his friend's specs. He confirmed the money was in his bank account and boxed up the computer for shipment the next day.

Not bad for a night's work. A few hundred bucks extra was certainly enough to treat his family to a pizza the next evening and enough left over to pay the electric bill. He considered what ACTION could have done on the stock market in the same time period.

His thoughts wondered about next month. The extra dough from friends to build computers was great, but not consistent enough. Hardly reliable. Just enough to cover a few past due bills when they came around.

It was almost one in the morning. He was tired. He skulked to his computer workstation to turn off the monitors so he could get a good night's sleep. However, he lingered over the keyboard to ACTION.

Would you like to start another query?

Other than their day jobs, how did normal people make money, like real money?

The stock market, of course. He already got a taste of ACTION's day trading prowess. Maybe that wouldn't be a terrible place to start. Of course, it was people gambling on the stock

market that had at least been partially respon-
sible for why his family had lost their home; a
big reason he avoided Wall Street. Plus, didn't
you need tens of thousands of dollars to day
trade with?

He plotted out his expenses in his head.
Things were tight. He couldn't really afford to
lose any of it.

Something lingered in his mind, a subdued
excitement at what could happen if he threw
his money down and won.

He started typing onto the keyboard, but
paused when his query was done.

Was this unethical? Was it wrong of him to
use ACTION to make money on the market?

Of course not. It was exactly what the big
trading firms did every day. Big firms with millions of dollars they could afford to lose.

Mikey nervously pressed enter and the three
dots flickered on the screen.

He felt like the guy in Las Vegas at the
roulette table, dropping his last few dollars on
black. The sweat dripping from his forehead

knowing that if he lost this bet; he was hitch-hiking home.

Five

His boss must have woken up on the wrong side of the bed that day, because he was insufferable to Mikey his entire shift. It had really got on Mikey's nerves. He just wanted to cope with the painfully slow day on his own. Not deal with the prattling and complaints of his overbearing manager hovering over his shoulder.

When his lunch shift rolled around, he had never been more excited to eat a bologna and processed cheese sandwich in his life. Mostly because it would yield him a break, if just a short one, away from his boss.

He ate in silence on the smoking bench behind the store, taking his time to chew every soggy bite, as if each chew somehow slowed time before his shift would begin again.

Mikey had been checking his phone all morning whenever his manager wasn't watching. Specifically, he was checking his bank account. Still $3.00, the exact minimum amount required by his bank. The rest he had told AC-TION to use to day trade with.

He thought about how financially irresponsible he had been. Checking the financial websites, the reports discussed unusually high levels of volatility in the market. Day traders weren't panicking, yet.

The stock market was pretty much legalized gambling, he probably had better luck betting on black at the roulette table. After a couple hours of nothing, he had given up on it yielding anything at all.

He finished his sandwich and crumpled the plastic wrapping into a ball and chucking it towards the garbage can. He missed, and it bounced twice on the ground.

He groaned.

Fishing into his pocket, he went to check the time. There was a new alert on his phone. It was from his bank, a notice of deposit.

He tapped it and waited for his statement to load. It was the moment of truth.

Mikey stared at his screen, unable to speak, for a long time.

It was so long that he had missed the start of his afternoon shift, and his manager was approaching him with a pissed-off look on his face.

"Do you know what time it is?" The angry little man asked, not expecting an answer. "You should have been back at your desk ten minutes ago."

Mikey didn't reply. He didn't even really hear him.

"Your generation is all alike," Mikey's boss continued. "Glued to your phones, nonchalant about responsibility. This country is going to hell in a handbasket and it's all because of people like you. You bet I'm going to finish writing you up for being late yesterday. Don't blame me, you're doing this to yourself."

He was huffing and puffing by the end of it, Mikey still not noticing him in the slightest.

"Do you have anything to say for yourself?" His manager asked in a way that indicated he didn't care for a thoughtful response.

Mikey looked up at him.

"I quit," Mikey said.

"You can't quit," his manager replied. "You're on the clock right now and corporate policy requires at least two weeks' notice if you ever want to be eligible for re-employment."

"I quit," Mikey repeated before adding. "Effective ten minutes ago."

He took off his name badge and placed it on the bench before standing up and walking away.

"Wait," his manager pleaded. "I need you at the desk. I don't know how to do any of this."

Mikey didn't stop, he just kept walking.

Not my problem.

The pizza they ate for dinner was delicious, exactly like Mikey remembered. Even better was that they were eating on ceramic plates instead of paper ones. Not exactly a night out at the Ritz, but it was quite the fancy feast by his family's meager standards. His mother had initially rejected his offer to pick up pizza again, but he had refused to listen. Mikey didn't want to tell her he had almost half a million dollars sitting in his checking account. She wasn't ready to know that. Instead, he told her he had won some money on a scratcher, that would be enough for her.

She would, of course, question the packages being delivered to the front door, scheduled for the next day. Mikey knew he would have to come up with a better excuse. He hoped that when she opened them to find the missing porcelain figures from her collection that they had lost in the move, that maybe she wouldn't be as critical of how he had come by enough money to afford such things. He didn't care, he just wanted his old mother back.

Mikey was feeling good. ACTION had given him and his family another inch of happiness, and he was determined to extend it into a mile.

He collected the plates and silverware from the table.

"Thank you, dear," his mother said, rubbing his arm.

"No problem, ma," he replied.

His dad let out a content grunt as he rubbed his protruding belly. With his skinny body and full, round stomach, he looked like a snake that had swallowed a melon. He couldn't move his face to smile at Mikey. Most of his dad's facial muscles were still paralyzed from the stroke, but his grunt was gratification enough.

Mikey rinsed the plates in the sink and load them into the dishwasher.

"Oh, you have to do them by hand, dear," his mother said from the table.

"Why's that?" Mikey asked, pulling out the plate he already placed inside.

"It's broken," she clarified.

"Oh," Mikey said, it wasn't exactly news to him that something in their rundown home wasn't working.

"How long has it been broken for?" Mikey asked, scrubbing away at the utensils with the sponge.

"A month," his mother replied.

He dropped the plate he was holding, and it clattered to the bottom of the basin.

"Are you alright, dear?" His mother asked, her face concerned.

"I'm fine," Mikey said, holding back the growing anger. "Did you tell the building manager already?"

"I did," she answered. "But you know him. He always tells us the same old thing. He'll get to it when he gets to it."

Mikey's fists clenched, the sponge in his hand oozing the white foam of the dish soap until it dripped like their leaky faucets.

He finished the dishes quickly and told his parents' good night, claiming he had to work on a few things late.

Of course, Mikey could have ordered a new dishwasher to be delivered the next morning. He had more than enough money. But to him, it was the principle of the thing. The property company that owned their home never made repairs. Their faucets had been leaking for months. They used the coin wash down the street for the last year because the washing machine in the unit was always broken. The cracks in the walls got wider every time it rained, and he was almost certain the basement had a hidden colony of mold growing somewhere.

They could move, they would move now that he had some money to make it happen. Still, someone else would move in, another family just as down on their luck as his. They'd get stuck in the same crappy situation as them, except they wouldn't have some magical A.I. program to make them hundreds of thousands of dollars in passive income.

He walked up to his workstation and unclenched his fists long enough to type out his query onto the screen and hit enter.

ACTION would take care of the rest.

The waiting room for his dad's doctor was about as boring and non-descript as they came. Mundane pastel paintings on the wall, generic magazines that were years past original publication, even the white tile floors, gave him a feeling as if he was waiting on a giant sterile wound pad.

Still, it was better than sitting at home. A city inspector had stopped in the day before for a 'random' inspection of the subsidized low-income housing, something they had never bothered to do in the years. The inspector ended up running out of paper to log all the violations found on the property.

The building manager stopped by shortly after; his tone strangely affected from being his usual confrontational and aggressive self to being apologetic and fearful. The workmen had been in and out of their place ever since. A plumber to work on the leaking pipes, delivery men with a shiny new dishwasher, and a restoration crew working on replacing the water damage and clearing out the mold in Mikey's basement.

With the loud noise and likeliness of exposure to toxic spores, Mikey had elected to join his father and mother at the doctor's office. They had been gone almost half an hour, inside talking to the doctor running the trial. Mikey had read through all the magazines already and his mind wandered to what he would use ACTION for when he got home.

The news played on the television.

Home sweet home, he thought of his mother glued to the couch.

He did his best to ignore it. The newscaster was talking about how the government was being accused of mismanaging funds for medical grants allotted for cancer research. Something he had little interest in.

The door to the backrooms of the medical facility opened and Mikey looked up, but when seeing it was a man walking out alone and not his parents, he quickly turned his eyes back to the floor and his thoughts. He was so preoccupied he didn't hear the man's footsteps grow louder.

His concentration only broke when the man's black leather shoes were in view, forcing Mikey to look up.

"Mikey?" the unfamiliar voice asked.

The man was about Mikey's age, and in great shape. He wore a nice suit jacket with a tan button-down shirt underneath. He didn't recognize the voice at all, but the face looked vaguely familiar to him.

"It's Tommy," the man said, smiling. "Tommy Thornton, from high school?"

The bulbs in Mikey's head lit up. He remembered Tommy, except he had a different nickname for him back when they were in school together. Back then, he was Tommy the Troll.

Tommy had practically terrorized Mikey when he was younger; zip tying him to hand rails, locking him in the girls' locker room, and stealing his lunch just to name a few. In fact, if there was one person on the planet Mikey would have preferred to never see again, of all the people that have crossed him, it was Tommy the Troll who would have been that person.

"Hi Tommy," Mikey said, struggling to find the words.

"What the hell are you doing here?" Tommy asked. "Hope you're doing ok."

"Just here with my folks," Mikey replied. "My dad had a stroke a while back."

"Sorry to hear that," Tommy said in the same tone that everyone uses, repeated so many times it felt almost mocking.

"You seem to be healthy," Mikey said. "What about you?"

"Here for a check-up," said Tommy. "I'm working at my dad's law firm downtown. It was pretty stressful for a while. Had a heart attack about a year ago."

"I'm sorry to hear that," Mikey replied in the same tone that Tommy had used, except he only hoped that Tommy hadn't recovered so well.

"But they fixed me up good," he said, pulling his shirt buttons apart to reveal several LED lights affixed to his chest. "They hooked me up with this new pacemaker, experimental. It's gonna be the wave of the future, hooked up to wi-fi, the next stage in the internet of things. I can see how well my heart is doing from an app now. Crazy right?"

"Crazy," Mikey repeated.

"Now I'm fit as a fiddle," said Tommy, putting his fists up like a boxer. "Doctor just said so."

"Happy to hear that," Mikey lied.

"Your folks still live off of Montgomery Street?" Tommy asked.

"No, we had to move a few years back," Mikey began. "We are living on the south side of town now."

"We, huh?" Tommy said with a sly smile.

Shit, Mikey hadn't meant to say it like that.

"Sounds like you're still the same old computer nerd I remember from back in the day," Tommy said. "Playing dungeons and dragons in the basement with your other wizard friends."

The same old nerd you used to stuff into a locker for fun.

"Pretty much," Mikey said, holding back his frustration.

Tommy didn't seem to notice.

"Well, it was good catching up," he said. "I'm grabbing a drink at BarFly later with a lady friend. You want to come?"

Why, so you can torment me for sport to impress her?

"I've got plans, but thanks," Mikey said. "I heard their martini is pretty good."

"The best," Tommy said. "Take care Mikey."

Mikey nodded.

Tommy left out the automatic sliding doors that lead to the parking lot.

Mikey remained holding back his anger. Every suppressed memory of school and Tommy the Troll rushing through his mind like a nightmare montage.

When they got home, the workmen tried to warn Mikey to not go into the basement yet. They weren't done. Mikey brushed them off and ripped open the plastic liner that protected his workstation from the spores and dust. He had to do one thing first, then he'd go back upstairs. He typed into ACTION's keyboard.

Make my old classmate Tommy Thornton move back in with his parents.

It took almost a week, but the workmen eventually finished and their lives got back to normal. Mikey had told his mother he started a new job working remote, and that it paid more. She was ecstatic for him and only slightly suspicious when he had waffled on telling her the name of the company. The more he lied, the harder it would be to keep them straight, so being vague and avoiding answering specifics would be his go-to strategy.

In his basement, he sat in front of two monitors.

On the left one was a live news feed from Bloomberg. On the right was ACTION's prompt screen, the familiar three dots indicating it was still working on his last query. Mikey watched Bloomberg's news ticker with intensity. He had been waiting patiently for almost two days. Nothing had happened yet, and like always, the impatient part of him was doubting ACTION's abilities. His doubt would prove unfounded.

"Breaking news," the Bloomberg anchor announced as they cut mid-feed from some pre-recorded business analyst's segment and went live.

"Pharmaceutical conglomerate Mendacium-Rx," the anchor continued. "Has just announced it is shutting its doors effective immediately. The company had long been the center of controversy after being indicted by a federal whistleblower for defrauding consumers. However, just in the last few hours, company operations have been immobilized as a cyber attack released millions of internal emails and documents to governments worldwide detailing not only fraudulent but other criminal activities ranging from human trafficking to tax evasion. Their assets have been frozen and their stock has plummeted from over $300 per share to less than a penny. Adding insult to injury, the police raided the home of the majority shareholders this morning finding evidence of child pornography on the personal computers of every member of the family who are, as we speak, being arraigned on charges."

In his excitement, Mikey smacked the armrest of his chair hard enough to make his palm sore.

"The news is sending shockwaves through the stock market and the Dow is in turmoil," the anchor added. "This comes just weeks after the market received another disruption when a yet unknown investor had heavily manipulated the Tokyo Index in the late hours of the night. Almost everything is in freefall. Bears with short positions are just raking in the money."

Mikey checked his bank account on his phone. The page loaded painfully slow as he almost salivated in anticipation.

When it finished, the amount of digits that in his checking account balance were longer than the small mobile screen could display.

He leaned back in his chair and yelled out triumphantly.

Turning to the screen with ACTION's prompt on it, the three dots had disappeared.

Where the results of the query satisfactory?

Can they trace the stock shorts back to me?

Very unlikely, the short positions were distributed in small batches using dummy corporations.

Mikey breathed a deep sigh of relief.

Then the results were satisfactory.
Would you like to start another query?

What at first had been an unsettling feeling watching ACTION at work had turned into delightful glee.

"Mikey," said a voice from the top of the stairs.

"Can't talk right now, ma," he yelled back. "I'm working."

"Can you come up here for a minute, please?" She asked.

"Not now, ma," he yelled again.

He grunted out loud when he heard her footsteps trudging down the stairs. He considered hiding his computer screens from view, but his mother was too ancient to understand what he was really doing.

"Sorry to intrude while you're working," she said solemnly as she approached his desk. "I was just talking on the phone to an old friend of mine. By the way, thank you for getting the landline hooked back up."

Mikey faked a smile and nodded. He was only half listening.

"Well, my friend still lives in the old neighborhood and she told me something," his mother's voice hesitated. "Something unfortunate about an old friend of yours. Do you remember Tommy Thornton?"

How could he not? He still has nightmares about the swirlies.

"I do," Mikey replied.

"Well, he had an accident," she continued. "He had some new heart implant thing, it was connected to the internet, lit up with all sorts of fancy circuit."

Mikey remembered Tommy had shown it off like he was Robert Downey Jr. in Ironman.

"Well, it failed," she said after a moment's hesitation.

"That's too bad," Mikey said, the apathy in his voice almost palpable.

"Apparently he lost oxygen to his brain for too long so now he's," she struggled to think of what to say. "What do you call it when your body is still functioning but your brain is not?"

"A vegetable," said Mikey immediately. Any sympathy he had for Tommy the Troll had been beaten out of him a long time ago.

"I wouldn't quite say that, but yes," his mother finished. "You know how religious his parents are, so they are having him transferred home to take care of him. He'll need a feeding tube and respirator for the rest of his life."

"That all?" Mikey asked.

"I know it's hard to hear the news," she said, patting on his shoulder.

It wasn't.

"I know you guys were close back in school," she continued. "If you want someone to talk to about it, I'm here to listen."

"No thanks," Mikey said. "I'm good."

He turned his attention back to his computer screens, specifically the one with Bloomberg Live, where the vulturous newscasters talked over each other in a feeding frenzy of excitement over the market.

His mother got the hint. She headed back up the stairs, but stopped halfway.

"You know it's really too bad," she said.

Mikey wanted to groan out loud, but held it back.

"That medical device was supposed to save a bunch of people's lives," his mother continued. "They are pulling it from the market entirely."

"Sure ma," Mikey replied. He wasn't really listening anyway, and he was happy to hear her close the door behind her as she left.

It had taken 7 days, but in that time period ACTION had completely dismantled a corporate empire, converted its demise into Mikey's immense personal gain, defeated his childhood arch enemy, and made him millions of dollars.

He felt something he hadn't in a long time, maybe never. He felt powerful.

Was there anyone who could stand in his way?

The rush filled him with inspiration.

Mikey started the list.

The list began with a word Mikey put little thought into, his emotions commanding his fingers as they typed on the keyboard.

Destroy...

The list continued on. It was extensive. His mind worked faster than he had ever thought possible. The names of companies and people seemed to pour from his memories like water from a faucet.

It comprised anyone who had ever crossed him personally, or he had heard about on the news for getting away with doing something wrong. It had corporate CEOs like Brendan Fowler, who had laid off thousands of blue-collar workers in order to bump his stock price and reap a substantial bonus. Politicians like the Governor who betrayed the public trust; valuing the voice of billionaire donors more than his constituents. Media personalities like Dale Vogelbrek who spun and twisted the truth until it drove others to hate and violence. International conglomerates that polluted our bodies for profit. Hell, he even added those who thrive on the price of a barrel of oil.

By the time he was done, he was breathing hard and sweating. The list spanned three lengths of the monitor's screen. Like Santa Claus, he had made a naughty list, and he was checking it twice. Finally going to give their due to those who were naughty at the detriment of the nice.

Surely the results would create a world where the wealth was more equally distributed to the poor like him and his parents. Well, previously poor.

He pressed enter.

Except this time, the three dots didn't appear right away.

This is an extensive query and may take a longer than the usual time to complete. Are you sure you would like me to proceed?

He thought for a moment about a response, and only one thing came to mind.

Take all the time you need. :)

The three dots appeared on the screen. AC-TION was going to work.

He felt a wave of exhaustion hit him as the adrenaline wore off. He crawled into his bed and closed his eyes.

He woke up the next day and went upstairs to find his mother cooking breakfast in the kitchen. He felt bad for how he had spoken to her the night before. She was making sausage and eggs, his favorite as a kid; so maybe she didn't feel right about it either. Whatever it was, neither dared speak it out loud.

"Morning, sweetheart," she said with a smile. "I tried the new card you gave me at the store yesterday and just like you said it would, it worked!"

"That's great, ma," Mikey replied, happy to see her feeling relief from their financial worries. "Did the Doctor call?"

Mikey sat down at the table next to his father, who was eating his eggs slowly, savoring it like he was afraid it would be his last home cooked meal.

"They can start treatments next week," she began. "They think he's a prime candidate."

"That's great, dad," Mikey said, putting his hand on his father's shoulder who nodded and smiled back, a little egg yolk dribbling from his chin.

"The delivery driver dropped off a few boxes this morning," his mother said with giddiness in her voice. "I thought they had the wrong address at first, but..."

She was struggling to talk, tears in her eyes.

"I just don't know what to say," she managed. "Thank you dear, I know it's silly, but I missed my little treasures."

Mikey felt his own heart swell up, but he didn't dare show it. He resorted himself to smiling at her as she dropped a plate of steaming yummy goodness in front of him.

"I have to ask," his mom said with a hint of worry. "Where is this money coming from? You're not selling drugs, are you?"

"I promise, ma," Mikey said with confidence. "Nothing illegal, just good old-fashioned luck."

Mikey forked a link of sausage and, despite the risk of the third-degree burn, shoved it into his mouth.

"Well, that's wonderful," she said. "Lord knows we've needed a bit of that as of late."

"Don't you worry," Mikey reassured her with a muffled voice. His mouth was full. "I've got us covered from here on out."

"That's sweet of you," she replied, before adding. "I almost forgot."

Mikey's eyes perked up.

"Somebody called the landline for you today," she said.

"Who was it?" He asked.

"It was a girl," his mother answered. "I told her you were sleeping and that I could take a message, but she just hung up."

Shit, it must be Rachel. Who else could it be? Did that mean the FBI was onto him if she was calling his house?

"If she calls back," Mikey said, trying to hide the panic in his voice. "Don't tell her I'm home. Tell her I moved out."

"Alright," his mother said as she poured him a glass of orange juice. "Is everything ok?"

"It's fine," Mikey said nervously, sipping at the glass. "Just an old girlfriend."

His mother didn't look convinced. Parents had an internal lie detector with their own children that was hard to crack.

"I got to go," Mikey said, shoving the rest of the food on his plate into his mouth and chugging the glass until it was empty. "Breakfast was great."

"You're welcome," she replied. He was almost out the door when she called back out to him.

"Mikey," she said, as he paused. "Try to take it easy. You've earned it."

"Thanks ma," he replied, then he was out the door.

Six

Mikey walked down the street with a nervous stride, his eyes darting around for any signs of the FBI Agent. This time of morning it was pretty busy, familiar faces walking past but not acknowledging him. They were people he saw every day, but they were more or less strangers to one another. The city did that sometimes, a defensive aura of unfriendliness. They were probably perfectly nice folk, just trying to carve out their own safe space in the world like him and his family. But when you are competing for air in a drowning contest, any contact with your fellow contestants just drags you both further down.

A man that didn't look so familiar was standing at the corner. He was talking but held no phone in his hand. His eyes darted everywhere as he spoke. The street was too loud for Mikey to hear what he was saying. The hairs on the back of Mikey's neck stood on end.

Mikey started walking in the opposite direction, pausing every few steps to turn his head just enough to see if the talking stranger had moved. Something else caught his eye, though.

Ahead of him, a white panel van sat idling. Its red taillights lit up and toxic fog puffing out of its tailpipe.

Maybe Mikey had watched the Bourne Identity series one too many times, but as he walked past it, he felt the eyes of its driver watching him.

Could that be one of those FBI surveillance vehicles?

Mikey put his hoodie up to cover his face. Maybe it was too late.

Mikey wasn't certain what was Hollywood and what was real when it came to spy movies. He lived in America; he had rights and freedoms that were unimpeachable like everyone else. At least he thought he did. But if they thought he had the program, why wouldn't they just get a warrant and breakdown his door? A quick search downstairs and they would find the evidence clear as day. He wasn't exactly hiding it.

The panel van shifted into gear and pulled out onto the street, almost like it was following him.

He didn't want to take any chances.

Mikey disappeared down the alley to his side and hid behind a dumpster. Not daring to peek out at first for the risk of betraying his position. He listened, ready to hear the sounds of boot steps on the asphalt as a team of agents swarmed the alley looking for him. They never came.

All he heard was the sound of the van's exhaust backfire as it passed the alley and faded away. It hadn't stopped to look for him. His fear of being monitored by the FBI was all in his head.

Or that was just what they wanted him to think.

They wouldn't be the FBI if they weren't good at following people, and Mikey wasn't exactly trained in spy craft. Maybe it was just their attempt to lull him into a false sense of security when he felt spooked and ducked into the alley. Not that they needed a white panel van to track his movements. Mikey had been on WikiLeaks. He knew about all the different methods the government had of tracking people using their phone. Who needed a team of people following him when, like the rest of America, he refused to leave home without it?

Pulling his phone from his pocket, he threw it to the ground and smashed it with his shoe heel, just like in the movies. Except it took him a half dozen stomps just to crack the screen. He resigned himself to just pulling the battery out and tossing it in the dumpster before continuing on at a brisk pace deeper into the alley. He must have crisscrossed and zig-zagged over a dozen times before risking stopping to check behind him. No one was following him, at least no one he could see.

Emerging back onto a street that he didn't recognize, he sprinted across it to the small little park on the other side. Trees well secluded it and he needed a quiet place to think, but more importantly somewhere to rest. He was not used to this much cardio.

He sat on the park bench that faced the entrance and ducked his head to hide his face with the hood. The park was mostly empty except for a couple of soccer moms chatting as their children played on a swing set. Unless they were recruiting toddlers, it was unlikely they were FBI agents there to follow him.

His breathing slowed enough that he could hear the soccer mom's conversation.

"I think we are moving to my mom's for a bit," the blonde one said.

"Out in the suburbs?" The brunette replied. "Is it because of what's happening on the news?"

"Oh my god yes," the blonde exclaimed. "All those workers broke into that CEO's penthouse just three blocks away from us. If I had been out walking the dog, it could have been me caught by that mob."

"It's the internet's fault," the brunette proclaimed. "They all went on that message board talking about how Brendan Fowler laid them off just to bump the stock price. Well, some anonymous person posted his home address and look at what happened. Whomever was posting on those boards had worked the lot of them up until they were frothing at the mouth. It only took one of them to take it to far and kill him."

"Such animals," the blonde commented before noticing Mikey was staring at them, listening to them.

"Did you say Brendan Fowler?" Mikey asked.

Both gave him a strange look, and neither replied. They hurriedly herded their children into strollers and disappeared out of the park.

Holy crap, did I hear them say Brendan Fowler was dead?

That was a name, one of his names from his list. The guy he had read about on the news the day before.

The park was now empty except for him. Anxiety formed in the pit of his stomach. He thought back to his query, **Destroy**. That was the word he had used. It didn't occur to him it had multiple meanings. He had meant it more figuratively, hoping that Brendan Fowler would get a taste of what had happened to him and his family. He didn't mean for him to be killed.

The black hole forming in his gut only grew when he realized he was no longer alone in the park.

A long-legged woman had come running through the entrance. She wore stretch athletic attire that clung tightly to her thin body. She wore her brown hair in a ponytail. Mikey was still feeling very suspicious. Was she just another jogger, or did she work for the FBI?

His worry only grew as she slowed down and stopped in front of his bench. Placing her foot on the seat, she stretched. Of all the benches in the park, she chose to stretch on the one he was sitting at. Not exactly typical behavior for people who lived in a city of strangers.

"Do you mind?" She asked, her voice soft.

Mikey did his best not to make eye contact.

"No," he muttered.

"You run here often?" Her voice had a slight southern twang to it. He guessed she had moved to the city only recently and the urban dialect hadn't fully destroyed her original. Either that or she was working for the FBI and it was all just an act.

"No," he muttered again.

Why would she think I run? Then he realized he was wearing sweatpants, a hoodie, and after his jog through the alleys, had stained them both dark with perspiration.

She continued to stretch on the bench next to him, and Mikey couldn't resist the urge to study her slender legs. If she was wearing a wire or a firearm, she definitely didn't have anywhere to store it.

"I come here all the time," she said with her gentle voice intoxicating him. "Especially when it's nice out like today. It's just too bad they are going to tear this place down."

"Tear it down?" Mikey repeated.

"Local news isn't allowed to talk about it," the girl explained. "Their parent company is trying to keep it under wraps. But that whack job in the Governor's Mansion is trying to clear the land it for one of his real estate buddies to develop into another apartment complex. The same developer who owns all that subsidized low-income housing nearby but doesn't do diddly squat to make them livable."

"I know of them," Mikey replied. Of course he did. He and his family lived in one of the properties. He had acute firsthand knowledge of what diddly squat meant.

"Can you believe they are suing the city?" she continued. "For hitting them with a bunch of violations? Suing the city for 'falsifying complaint records'."

She had used air quotes but her southern accent going into hyper-drive as she said it would have done the trick.

"Somebody started this group online to march on the governor's mansion tonight," she added. "People seem pretty fired up about this whole thing. I've been reading all about it on..."

"A message board," Mikey finished her sentence for her.

"Oh, how'd you know?" She said, smiling at him. "Are you secretly one of us?"

Mikey wanted to smile, but his heart and his brain were moving in opposite directions.

"I got to go," he said, standing up.

"Don't let me hold up your run," the girl said, watching him. "Will I see you tonight at the protest?"

He wanted to say yes, if only to get to talk to her again and hear her sweet voice.

"Maybe," was all he managed.

Once Mikey was out of the park and running down the street, he ducked into a coffee shop. Partially because his lungs needed a break from the personal best 200ft he had just tried to run but also because his anxiety was increasing by the minute. He felt like he was going to throw up the delicious sausage and eggs his mother had made for him that morning.

Pulling on the bathroom door, the handle didn't budge.

"Paying customers only, sir," said a grumpy-looking barista.

Mikey had forgotten that the only money he had was in a bank account, only accessible from his phone. Taking deep breaths, he walked towards the exit. He was doing everything in his power to keep his heart rate and breakfast down. The television above the door blared the news.

"Right-wing firebrand Dale Vogelbrek was killed early this morning when his self-driving car seemingly ran itself off the road," the newscaster on the screen said. "Authorities aren't blaming faulty software officially, but his supporters suspect foul play was involved. Dale was recently fired from his hit prime-time talk show after the network took umbrage with his wild conspiracy theories of a secret cabal by the Illuminati to use A.I. to shape world events. His wife and two daughters were also in the vehicle and are currently in critical condition at a local hospital."

Mikey couldn't hold it any longer. He lunged for the nearest trashcan and vomited.

SEVEN

Mikey walked back to the door of his parents' house, no longer concerned about the FBI following him. There was no white panel van waiting on the street. His paranoia about them seemed completely unfounded after trying to destroy his phone and running the back alleys like he was in some Russian cold war spy movie. He felt tired, not just tired, exhausted. He shuffled slowly into the house.

For once, the news wasn't on in the living room. Mikey was thankful for that.

His mother was unpacking her various porcelain figures and arranging them in the display cases.

"How was your day?" She asked without looking up.

"Fine," he muttered in response.

"You don't sound fine," she said, turning to see him.

He was soaked with sweat, his eyes were dull, and his face was as white as a vampire.

"You must have come down with whatever is going around," she said, rushing to him.

"I'm really fine," he said, but it didn't sound convincing.

"Straight to bed," she ordered, escorting him to the basement door. "You get changed and I'll be right down with some soup."

"Ma, I'm really fine," he pleaded.

"Nonsense," she said like her old self. Part of that made him feel like a ten-year-old kid again. "To bed, now."

He obeyed her orders, his body feeling exhausted and his mind still trying to process the day's events.

A few minutes later, Mikey lay tucked in bed and his mother sitting bedside, stroking his hair. He could see the computer monitor for ACTION lit up at his desk, the three little dots flickering on the screen.

"I really need to work on something," he said, trying to sit up, but his mother stopped him.

"You are just going to rest," she told him, gently pushing him back down. "Whatever it is, can wait till morning."

What was he going to do, anyway? ACTION didn't have a pause or cancel button. He would just have to wait for it to run its course. He could try to unplug it, but that might just make it worse.

"Can I read you a bedtime story?" she asked him.

"Ma," he groaned.

"Oh, come on," she continued. "For old time's sake? Maybe The Fisherman and his Wife? You loved that one when you were a boy"

"I'm too old and too tired for stories," he said.

"Fine, suit yourself," she replied, standing up. "I'll be down to check on you in the morning."

"Alright," Mikey said.

She leaned down, and he moved his head to the side so she could kiss his cheek.

Ascending the stairs, she hit the light switch so that only the light from the open doorway above was visible behind her silhouette.

"I'm sorry I haven't been present the last few years to help you out," she whispered. "I sure appreciate you, Mikey."

Mikey couldn't hear her, because he was already fast asleep.

Mikey awoke the next morning feeling better. He must have slept a long time, because the light coming in from the small window was bright, like midday. He didn't know what time it was, his phone was probably on its way to the dump by now.

Pulling himself out of bed, he shuffled over to his workstation. It was almost noon, according to the little clock on the bottom right of the screen on ACTION's monitor. But there was something else on the screen as well.

Where the results of the query satisfactory?

Mikey's senses came to life immediately, like being splashed in the face with freezing cold water.

Pulling up the web browser, he typed in Brendan Fowler's name. The man's obituary pulled up immediately. The man, who had laid off thousands of people just to line his pockets, was dead. As well as five others that also lived in his building who were simply in the wrong place at the wrong time when the recently unemployed showed up in droves to give Brendan a piece of their mind.

Next, he searched for Dale Vogelbrek. The hot-headed public figure that had millions of followers online ready to do his every command, also dead. His wife following him to the afterlife after a valiant fight in the ICU, their two young daughters not far behind. A statement from the manufacturer of his self-driving car was quick to put out a press release that there was no evidence the vehicle's A.I. had been faulty. Vogelbrek's internet army didn't believe a word of it, their leader dying a martyr to the cause. They were planning a march on the factory, and if it would be anything like their past marches, it would quickly devolve into vandalism and violence.

Mikey didn't even have to type in the Governor's name to find the news article. The governor, who was cozy with big land developers, was another casualty; along with three members of his security detail and four protesters. A Pulitzer Prize worthy photo featured four bodies covered in sheets on a manicured lawn, bright flames behind them engulfing the Governor's mansion. One of the bodies caught his eye. It was long and slender under the sheet, almost a skeleton in shape. The end of a brown ponytail was visible sticking out of the top. He knew who it was immediately. It was the girl from the park.

One by one, down his query list, he checked each name. One by one, they all showed up in the news as dead or destroyed, each under different circumstances.

When Tommy the Troll had been turned into a vegetable, Mikey had felt no remorse. However, each one of these nameless people, bystanders of ACTION's machinations, all took a toll on him more than a million Tommy the Trolls ever would. He clicked to the main page of the news site and checked the headlines. None of the deaths even made the top five stories anymore.

STOCK MARKET IN FREEFALL, RETIREMENT SAVINGS FOR MOST WORKING CLASS AMERI-CANS COMPLETELY WIPED OUT

ANALYSTS PREDICT 40% UNEMPLOYMENT RATE BY XMAS, BEST CASE

US AND CHINA EXCHANGE MISSILES IN SOUTH CHINA SEA AS ECONOMIC PRESSURES OVER THE DISPUTED AREA'S RESOURCES HEAT UP

EXPLOSION AT SEED PROCESSING PLANTS KILLS 30, DESTROYS KEY RESEARCH. EXPERTS WARN OF COMING FAMINE AS NO REPLACE-MENTS FOR TERMINATOR SEEDS AVAILABLE FOR A LEAST A YEAR

OPEC DECIDES TO HOLD BACK 95% OF OIL EXPORTS CITING LOW MARKET PRICES, BLAME THE US GOVERNMENT FOR MANIPULATING THE MARKET

Mikey couldn't believe it; every headline was related to a person or company from his list. This was not what he thought would happen. He thought he would wake up to a world that felt more fair and just. He thought he was being Robin Hood, but the poor were more screwed now than they were before.

What did you do?

Mikey's fingers mashed into the keyboard, testing the limits of the cheap plastic's integrity.

`I completed the query according to the outcome requested.`

THEN UNDO IT!

The three dots appeared and sat there for a long while. Mikey kept hitting refresh on his news feed, hoping and begging for one piece of good news to pop up. The headlines read worse and worse each time. Looting, rioting, militant gangs; more and more violence was erupting by the minute across the country as the entire system fell apart.

The three dots disappeared at last. Mikey breathed a sigh of relief.

Unfortunately, I was unable to complete your last prompt. Please try again.

Mikey wanted to punch a hole through the screen. It couldn't reverse it? It could do anything. Why couldn't it reverse it?

He took a deep breath, trying to calm down.

The phone rang upstairs. He heard his mother answer.

Mikey tried to think of something to undo the damage. He thought about his own parents and the hundreds of millions of others like them who had saved up their entire lives through investments into 401ks and IRAs; forging their own path to retirement. All that money had just disappeared with the stock market in almost an instant.

Mikey's keystrokes grew less frantic. They slowed to a crawl; they had become desperate. The keys were slippery from his falling tears.

Just give the people back their money.

Three dots.

It didn't take more than three seconds for it to reply this time.

Unfortunately, I was unable to complete your last prompt. Please try again.

Mike began cursing at the top of his lungs, every obscenity he could think of. Screaming and shouting as he stomped around the room; kicking old computer towers and breaking everything he could get his hands on. The box of obsolete spare parts was an unfortunate casualty of his anger; their contents exploding into thousands of tiny little chips and resistors that scattered in every direction as it hit the floor with a crash.

If such words as regicide and homicide existed; surely the rage fueled act he was about to commit would be called computacide.

Holding ACTION's tower high above his head, he prepared to throw it to the concrete floor and snuff out whatever evil electronic entity was imprisoned inside.

He felt like he had made a pact with the devil when he had agreed to bring it home. It was his monkey paw, his magical fish, his genie's lamp.

"Honey," his mother said from the top of the stairs, her voice calm but concerned.

His mother's kind voice cleared his head.

"What?" he said in between breaths.

"Phone is for you," she said. "It's the girl again."

Mikey sat the computer down.

Maybe Rachel could fix this, undo whatever was done. She was smart; she knew the program, maybe she knew a way out of this mess.

"Do you still want me to tell her you moved?" Mikey's mother asked.

"No, it's ok," Mikey replied. "I need to talk to her."

Mikey walked up the stairs. His shirt and hair were both soaked with sweat.

"Ok dear," his mother said as he passed her at the top of the stairs. She held her hand over her mouth to hold back a gasp.

The landline was off the hook and sitting on the kitchen table, Mikey picked it up.

"Rachel," he said, almost out of breath.

"Mikey, is that you?" Her familiar voice replied.

"Yes, yes, it's me," he stammered. The adrenaline was wearing off and his muscles were shaking.

"Do you still have the computer?" She asked, her voice hinting at the slightest bit of desperation.

Mikey wasn't certain he should answer.

"It's ok, just tell me," she said after waiting. "Do you still have it?"

Mikey didn't want to admit it. He didn't want to take responsibility. Because it wasn't his fault, it was Rachel's. She was the one who created ACTION; she was the one who had given it to him. Rachel was the real villain.

"Yes," Mikey said, anger growing in his voice. "You should have told me what it was."

Rachel paused for a moment, Mikey thought it was suspicious.

"I did," she eventually said. "I told you it was A.I. and I told you not to use it. You used it, didn't you?"

She wasn't wrong. Mikey did kind of break the rules. Maybe he was a little at fault for what was happening.

"I tried to use it to fix things," he said.

"This is you fixing things?" Rachel said, almost with a laugh. "The world is falling apart, and that is you fixing things."

"I wanted to make things right," said Mikey defensively. "The government, these big businesses; they step on us every day. I wanted to give them a taste of their own medicine."

He could hear Rachel sigh on the other side of the line.

"You're right, they do," she said, her tone changing dramatically. She sounded more soft and empathetic than he had ever heard her before. "But some things in this world, you can't just change overnight. You can't flip the table just because you're pissed off you drew a shitty hand."

Mikey didn't know what to say.

"Maybe we can still fix this," Rachel said, breaking the silence. "Where is it now?"

"It's downstairs in the basement," he said, the fight in him snuffed out. Mikey just wanted to do what was right, give it back to her, and let her put out the fire he had set on the planet.

Rachel didn't reply right away.

"There you got it," she said to someone not on the line. "The program is in the basement. He's not near it. You can move in now."

"What? Who are you talking to?" Mikey asked with confusion.

"I warned you Mikey," she scolding, her tone changing back to the Rachel he remembered. "But you just didn't want to listen, did you?"

"You didn't warn me I had some all powerful, world killing, demonic A.I. in my basement?!" He was yelling into the phone, but there was no one there to listen. The line was dead.

The kitchen window glass broke as a canister came flying into the room. Before he could react, the flashbang went off and Mikey hit the ground disoriented. His head pulsated with every heartbeat. The world around him clouded in fog. The ringing in his ears felt like someone was driving nails into his eardrums.

Dark figures moved around in the dense, gray cloud, one landing on top of Mikey as he laid sprawled on the floor. He struggled to find breath as he felt the wind knocked out of him; the smoke filling his lungs with each gasp. He thought for a moment he was going to suffocate.

He felt many hands on him, grabbing and pulling at him in different directions like they were trying to pull him apart limb from limb.

Details formed in the room, another figure lay on the floor a few yards away. The frizzy white hair of his mother was recognizable immediately, she wasn't moving. She looked like a corpse prop for an action movie, or maybe she was just innocent bystander number four; just as slow as three had been. He felt a painful feeling in his heart, worry that she might be dead.

He tried to scream out, but his lungs failed him and all he could do was cough and choke on his own breath.

He struggled to breathe until he passed out from the effort.

When he awoke again, the kitchen was full of bright light. The curtains that usually covered the window laid on the tile floor, allowing a few rays of sunshine to burst forth into room unimpeded. He felt like he had just woken up from the worst hangover of his life. His whole body ached, his lungs and throat burned, and his skull felt like some little man was trying to jackhammer his way out of it.

He tried to roll over onto his back but couldn't. His hands were zip-tied together behind him and so were his legs; they were so tight he didn't think Harry Houdini could have escaped from them.

Mikey tried to squirm, but felt a sharp pain as something on the ground cut his cheek. A pool of blood grew on the tile, shards of glass dotting it like islands in a sea of red.

He remembered the last thing he could, his mother lying face down, looking dead.

"Mom, where are you?" A heaving cough interrupted his yell, but the words came out, nonetheless.

No response.

"Ma!" He yelled again, this time with less pain than before.

"Your mom is fine," said a man appearing in the doorway. He was dressed in full SWAT gear, but from Mikey's perspective, he couldn't see much more than that.

"Where is she?" Mikey asked in between another fit of coughing.

The man in the SWAT gear ignored him.

"Suspect is awake," the SWAT officer said into the radio mounted to his chest.

Mikey's feeling of relief that his mother was alright only made him feel better for a few seconds.

His tears splashed like boulders into the small crimson lake, forming on the tile under his face.

"Stop crying. Be a man," the officer told him with a scoff.

"I'm not crying," Mikey replied. He either didn't know or didn't want to admit that tears were streaming down his face.

The man in SWAT gear knelt down over him and stuck a strip of duct tape over Mikey's mouth. Mikey struggled to breathe through his nose.

"Much better," the man said, standing back up. "My kids whine enough at home, shouldn't have to listen to punks like you do the same at work."

The man's radio made a loud beep.

"They're coming in," a voice on the radio said.

Mikey could see two more sets of feet appear in the doorway and enter the kitchen.

One was a pair of black oxfords with slacks. The man was wearing a suit.

"Do me a favor and tell your boys downstairs not to touch anything," the familiar voice said. "The FBI liaison will be the one to search the basement for it."

"You got it," the SWAT said as he stepped into the hallway and out of sight.

Mikey remembered the familiar voice. He didn't need to see the man's face to picture it in his mind. It was the face that he had been imagining was lurking in the shadows the day before. It was the man from the black SUV. The one who had interrogated him on the street near the dungeon. It was the FBI agent.

Mikey recognized the other pair of feet as well, sneakers with white socks and gray sweatpants.

"I still can't believe this twerp and a computer are causing this whole goddamn mess," the Agent said with disdain.

"Well, maybe if you hadn't come after me like the KGB, I wouldn't have given it to him," Rachel said, her voice fresh in Mikey's mind after hearing her on the phone before the flashbang had gone off.

"I thought we were being rather nice about it, considering you had a doomsday device," the Agent replied. "Any idea what this guy used it for?"

"I don't know," Rachel said, brushing the glass on the ground next to Mikey's face away with her shoe. The blood smeared with it. "Must have thought he was Robin Hood or something."

"I thought you were playing us," the agent said.

"I wasn't," she said. "Once I saw the news, I knew he had to be stopped."

"You really think he would have destroyed it, or worse, used it one last time if we had knocked on the front door with a warrant?" The agent asked.

"Maybe, maybe not," Rachel replied. "Wasn't worth risking either way. Told you my plan would work with minimal collateral damage."

"Well, I talked to the brass," the agent began. "They aren't happy about the whole thing, but they appreciate you helping us find him. If the machine can cause this kind of havoc, they are interested if it can be used for more constructive purposes. I think you've proven capable. Are you ready to join the team?"

"Do I have a choice?" Rachel replied.

"I hear the weather in Guantanamo ain't half bad this time of year," the FBI Agent said dryly.

"I'm sure he'll be able to tell me all about it," Rachel said with a snicker. "Poor schmuck shouldn't have turned it on. I warned him."

"Well, if they listened to people like us more often," said the agent as he walked from the room. "They wouldn't be poor schmucks, then would they?"

"He seemed like a nice guy," Rachel remarked to no one in particular. She watched Mikey with sad eyes. "Down on his luck, but still a nice guy."

Mikey wriggled and squirmed as he listened. A helpless earworm. He tried to scream, but no sound came out. Either the duct tape was preventing him from doing so or he was crying too hard.

Rachel knelt over Mikey for a moment, pulling his hair from over his eyes as he struggled against the restraints.

"Sorry Mikey," she said. "The world is not fair sometimes, doesn't mean just anybody gets to change it."

She stood up and walked out, leaving only red footprints in her wake.

Now alone, the world of the kitchen had gone quiet. The only sounds he could hear were the sobs of his mother in the next room.

The world certainly was unjust, but maybe that's the way the world likes it.

THE END

C.R. Allen, an Arizona native, balances life as a dad, business professional, and a passionate author. A proud alumnus of Arizona State University, where he completed both his undergraduate and master's degrees, his fascination with storytelling began early, crafting his first screenplay at age 10. Today, he is known for his compelling novels, novellas, and short stories of horror, supernatural thrillers, and historical fiction. Allen's writings stand out for their dark and mysterious narratives that explore sociological, psychological, and technological themes.

Follow him on Social Media for updates on new releases, free early access to alpha books, and other fun content that fans of his work will love!

a, amazon.com/author/crallen

OVERCLOCKED

f facebook.com/crallenwrites/

instagram.com/c.r.allenwrites/

https://twitter.com/crallenwrites

tiktok.com/@crallenwrites

pinterest.com/crallenwrites/

youtube.com/channel/UCiqwmwwgIN9JUTwJDgl3KOA

goodreads.com/crallenwrites

bookbub.com/authors/c-r-allen